A Day with Your Dog

Wes Lipschultz

Rosen
REAL
READERS

The Rosen Publishing Group, Inc.
New York

1

Do you have a dog?

You can feed your dog.

You can walk your dog.

You can play with your dog.

You can run with your dog.

You can hug your dog.

Words to Know

feed

hug

play

run

walk